A Hug Goes Around

To Allan, with hugs
—L.K.M.

A hug for Susan Pearson
—B.L.

A Hug Goes Around
Text copyright © 2002 by Laura Krauss Melmed
Illustrations copyright © 2002 by Betsy Lewin
Printed in Hong Kong. All rights reserved.
www.harperchildrens.com

Library of Congress Cataloging-in-Publication Data
Melmed, Laura Krauss.
A hug goes around / by Laura Krauss Melmed / illustrated by Betsy Lewin.
p.   cm.
Summary: During the course of a busy day, family members continue to share
a hug by passing it on to others.
ISBN 0-688-14680-5 — ISBN 0-688-14681-3 (lib. bdg.)
[1. Hugging — Fiction.   2. Family life — Fiction.   3. Day — Fiction.
4. Stories in rhyme.]   I. Lewin, Betsy, ill.   II. Title
PZ8.3.M55155 Hu   2002   00-068194
[E]-dc21   CIP
                              J J Fic   AC

Typography by Al Cetta
1 2 3 4 5 6 7 8 9 10
❖
First Edition

A Hug Goes Around

By Laura Krauss Melmed

Illustrated by Betsy Lewin

■ HARPERCOLLINS*PUBLISHERS*

A mountain goes up.
A valley goes down.
Where does a hug go?
A hug goes around.

Rosy sun's risin'
In her pink gown.
Ma lifts the baby—

A hug goes around.

Sweet smells of breakfast
Drift up the stairs.
Down tumble children,
Hungry as bears.

Flapjacks go flip-flop.
Butter is found.

Syrup tips over—

A hug goes around.

Soapsuds go *slip-slop*,
Dishrag goes *swish*.

Lizzie's not looking—
Quick! Catch that dish!

Whee-ee-ee! Tom goes swinging.
Scree-ee-ee! wails the gate.
Don't let the chicks out!

Whoops! It's too late.

Pa's planting pole beans.
Tom yells, "Come see!"

Champ has chased Whisper
Up the oak tree!

Champ's in the doghouse,
But Tess is so brave,
She climbs up the oak tree~

And Whisper is saved!

Ma's going fishing.
Lizzie goes, too.
Now angry clouds threaten,
And Ma says, "We're through!"

Thunder comes CRASHing.
Raindrops pelt down.
Lightning is frightening!
A hug goes around.

The storm soon blows over,
Bright sun shines at last.
Four mud-puddle jumpers
Run wild in the grass.

The girls prance in turbans,
While—rub-a-dub-dub—
Tom and the baby
Are having a scrub.

Once supper is over,
Pa tickles the strings,
And Ma rocks the baby
While everyone sings.

Teeth are all toothbrushed.
Prayers have been said.

Children are snuggly,
Tucked into bed.

Sleep, ginger kitty.
Sleep, lick'rish hound.
Sleep, little darlin's.

A hug goes around.

Moon on the mountain.
Quiet abounds.

"Isn't peace sweet, dear?"

A hug goes around.